**PROMISES**

Yasmin's Journey

by Miriam Halahmy

Published by Ransom Publishing Ltd.

Unit 7, Brocklands Farm, West Meon, Hampshire GU32 1JN, UK

**www.ransom.co.uk**

ISBN       978 178591 256 6

First published in 2016

# Yasmin's Journey

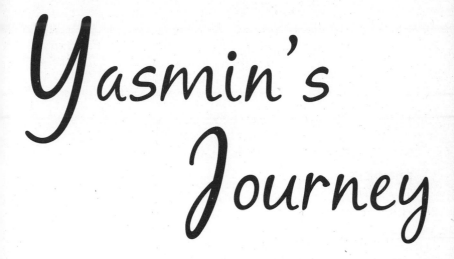

Miriam Halahmy

Rans⁕m

*For asylum seekers everywhere
who are seeking
a safe place to live.*

# ONE

## The Fun Girls

**The Fun Girls**

- Anyone bored?
- Me!
- Me too. 🙁
- I'm drawing my bed, how sad
  is that? 😣

'Yasmin,' calls Mum from the kitchen.

'Come and help with dinner.'

'Ok,' I call back.

I tap in, Bye now, and click my screen off.

It's not safe to go out after school, in case there's a bomb. So me and my friends send pics and stuff on What's App. We call ourselves *The Fun Girls*. We hate war and we love our phones.

The Fun Girls just want to have fun.


Our flat has three bedrooms and a big kitchen/living room. Ali's zooming round with his plane when I go in.

'Tat,tat,tat,tat!' he yells.

He plays war all the time. I hate it.

'Stop it, Ali,' I hiss.

He grins at me. 'Tat, tat, tat, Yas-min.'

I shake my fist at him, but Mum spots me and snaps, 'He's only six. Grow up girl!'

*I'm fifteen*, I think, *I am grown up*. But I keep quiet.

Dad gets home just after seven and we sit down for dinner. There's rice and a tiny bit of chicken.

Food's short because of this horrible war. Ali misses sweets and so do I, but I don't say so; it's babyish.

Dad says we have to put up with things now. I try, but it's so hard.

I dream of what my life will be like when the war's over, going to my friends' homes and staying up late. I want to be a teacher when I leave school.

After dinner I make tea. Ali puts a spoon of sugar in his cup and then takes one more.

'That's too much,' says Dad.

'Just tonight,' says Mum, and she and Dad look at each other.

*Something's wrong*, I think.

Then Dad says, 'Yasmin, Ali, listen to me. The war's very bad and life's getting more and more dangerous. The flats at the park were bombed last night.'

'That's so near to us!' I gasp.

Dad nods. 'We can't stay here any longer. You are leaving tomorrow with your Mum.'

'Leaving our flat?' says Ali.

'Leaving Syria,' says Dad, 'for a new life where it's safe.'

'What about you?' I say.

'I'm going ahead tonight to someone who will help us,' says Dad.

*No way!* I think.

'I don't want to go,' I say. 'What about school and all my friends?'

'That's not important now,' says Dad.

'When will we come home?' asks Ali with a sob.

'Never,' says Dad, and Mum starts to weep too.

# TWO

## On the Road

'Wake up Yasmin. It's time to go.'
Mum shakes me.

It's still dark, only 3.00 am.
I packed my bag last night. I put in
clothes, a book and my phone. So
the Fun Girls can message me.
I HATE going away from them.

I dress in jeans and a top and

11

cover my hair with a brown *hijab*.
Then I go out of my room. Ali is
kicking his bag.

'Mum won't let me take my
Jedis!' he shouts.

Ali has 14 Jedis. He's Star Wars
mad, so I have to think fast.

'Take your best one and give me
one for my bag,' I say.

He runs in his room and comes
back with two toys. He gives me
one and makes sure I push it deep
in my bag.

'Come on, children. We must go –
but be very quiet. We don't want
anyone to hear us,' says Mum.

'Like who?' asks Ali in a loud voice.

'Shush,' I say. 'You know. ISIS.'

That shuts him up. We are all scared of ISIS. They are so bad. They kill people just for wearing the wrong clothes or looking at them the wrong way.

Outside the June air is cool, but it will be hot later. Mum gave me three bottles of water and a bag of food, so now my backpack is very heavy.

We walk and walk until we leave

the town behind. The sun comes up and the road goes through rocky hills. Other people overtake us with heavy bags. No one speaks. Everyone's scared.

We pass a village, but it looks empty.

'My feet hurt,' says Ali. 'I want to stop.'

'No,' says Mum. 'Not until we get to Dad.'

'But I'm tired!' shouts Ali.

People on the road turn and stare. I'm tired too, but I tell Ali to SHUT UP!

Then someone points at the sky.

We all look up. A plane is coming closer and closer.

'Hide!' a man shouts. 'He will bomb us for running away!'

Mum grabs me and Ali and pulls us into a ditch by the road.

Ali screams out, 'I dropped my Jedi!'

I look back. His toy is lying face down in the dirt.

Then the sky explodes. Rocks and sand and bits of trees fly all around us.

I hug Ali and Mum, shaking with fear. We are going to die! I am only fifteen.

But the plane flies on.

We get up and see a huge hole

in the road, but no one was hurt.

'My Jedi, my Jedi!' Ali shouts. 'He's gone. The bomb killed him, Yas-min.'

Ali is crying and looking up at me. I am his big sister, but I can't fix this.

I take his hand and say to Mum, 'We must go. Now!'

We hurry around the big hole and back onto the road.

*Don't look back*, I think. Your life in Syria is over. We are going to a new country and a new life.

But my heart feels like a rock inside.

16

# THREE

## *All Grown Up*

It is dark by the time we get to Dad's friend, Hassan. We are so tired and hungry.

But Hassan has bad news. 'Your Dad is not here.'

'Did he send a message?' asks Mum, her eyes wide with fear.

Hassan shakes his head.

Hassan makes tea and gives us some cold rice and beans. Ali's eyes close after he eats. Hassan shows us to a bed in the corner. I lie down next to Ali and wait for Mum.

When she comes her voice is very sad.

'I must go back, Yasmin, and find Dad. You and Ali go to the border. It's only one more day to walk. Dad and I will meet you in Turkey.'

My heart turns to ice. 'No, Mum! Not without you. I'm too scared.'

But Mum won't listen. 'You

have to go and you have to look after Ali. You are a big girl now, Yasmin.'

Am I? How did that happen in one day?

She turns over and goes to sleep, as tears fall down my cheeks.


I am terrified of going on without Dad and Mum. I'm only fifteen.
I can't look after myself, let alone a six-year-old.
What if Ali gets sick or breaks his leg?

I need *The Fun Girls* to cheer me up.

**The Fun Girls**

- Hey Yas ... what's up?
- You weren't in school today
- Fatima B and Fatima K messed up their maths and had to clean the toilets
- Yurrk! Sick!!!

I grin, but Dad said I mustn't say anything online in case ISIS read it and come looking for us. I miss my friends so much, but I don't message them back.

We wake up a few hours later. It's still dark. I pull on my clothes and cover my hair with my *hijab*.

Maybe Mum will change her mind this morning.

'Listen,' I say. 'We can come back with you to find Dad ... '

'No!' Mum says. 'It's not safe. Take this.' She hands me a money belt. 'Put it round your waist. Don't let anyone see it. That is all our money to escape Syria.'

Then she kisses us and pushes us out of the door. 'Go! And take care of Ali.'

My legs start to shake – but what can I do? Ali is holding the last Jedi toy. I take his hand and we walk off down the road.

Now *I* am the grown up. How mad is that?

The sky gets light and the sun comes up. We walk and walk, following a big group of people. When they stop to rest, we stop too. We eat a piece of bread and sip our water. No one talks to us or looks at us.

I hear a man say, 'Not far to go, my son.' I look round. He is patting a boy's head.

I wish he was my dad, keeping me and Ali safe.

Feeling angry, I tug Ali's hand hard. 'Come *on*!'

'Ok!' Ali shouts back.

We are both tired and sad and scared.

Everyone walks until it is very dark, but we do not stop. Then I see a light up ahead.

'The border!' someone shouts.

'Turkey! We are safe, *inshallah*,' cries out a woman.

Ali and I wait in line for a long time. Ali nearly falls asleep standing up. Then a man in a uniform with a gun on his belt snaps, 'Passport!'

I hold out our passports. My

heart thumps like a drum. What if he won't let us in?

He says something to a man behind him. Then he turns back, sniffs and stamps our papers.

'*Yallah*. Go on!' He pushes us through a gate.

We are in Turkey.

I hug Ali and he yells, 'Let the Force be with us!'

Now all we need is Mum and Dad.

# FOUR

## Kamal

The camp is full of people and rows
of big tents. We stand there all
alone and I have no idea what to
do.

Then a woman calls, 'Hey, you
kids!'

She gives us two bottles of
water, a small bag of food and two

blankets. She takes us to a tent and says, 'Find a place to sleep.'

We go inside. It's mad in there; hundreds of people, babies screaming, kids running around, women shouting. My head is spinning with the noise.

Ali tugs my hand. 'Over there, Yas.'

We find a small space at the side and lay down on our blankets. I am so tired I fall asleep.


When I wake up it is light, and for a moment I don't know where I am. Then I look for Ali. He's not here.

Oh God! What will Mum say?

I jump to my feet, shouting, 'Ali! Ali!' and run outside.

The sun is up and the light blinds me. There are so many people and so much noise.

Where is he?

My phone is in my hand and I almost message *The Fun Girls*, but what can they do?

Then a voice calls, 'Yas! Over here! Meet my friend.'

It's Ali and he's grinning at a boy my age.

'This is Kamal. He *LOVES* Star Wars!'

Ali and Kamal bump fists and throw the Jedi toy between them.

It's very stupid, but I'm so glad Ali is safe I don't care.

'Hello Kamal,' I say, feeling very shy.

*The Fun Girls* don't talk to boys at home. It is not allowed. But we talk *about* them of course.

Kamal is taller than me, with shaggy hair. He's wearing jeans and carrying a phone.
'Hi,' he says and he sounds shy too.
'I need a charger. Want to come along?'

That's just what I need – and then I can ring Mum.

We follow Kamal through the camp to a tent. Inside there is a table and phone chargers. I plug mine in.

'Ali told me you got here last night,' said Kamal. 'I've been here two months.'

'With your family?' I say.

He shakes his head and his big eyes are so sad.

'Alone.'

I don't know what to say. Kamal walks off. But he comes back with some bread and water to share with us.


As we eat, Ali chatters on. 'The toilets stink and there's only one tap. I don't have to wash, do I Yas?

Everyone says they want to go to Germany, right Kamal?'

Kamal gives him a kind smile.

'When will Mum and Dad be here?' Ali goes on. 'Tell them to bring the two Jedi on my pillow. Please, Yas.'

'OK, OK, but shut up now,' I say.


When my phone is charged I tap in Mum's number.

It rings for ages and then Mum says, 'Yasmin! Where are you? Is Ali safe?'

'Yes, Mum. We're in Turkey, in the camp. When are you and Dad coming?'

Silence. I wait.

Then she says, 'Dad was shot in the street. He's in hospital.'

'What?!?'

Ali tugs my arm. I push him away.

'Listen, Yasmin, darling,' Mum says. 'You must get to Greece. It's not safe in the camp. We will come in a few days when Dad's better. Go on … '

The phone breaks up.

' … Greece … '

'Mum!' I scream, but she's gone.

I look at Kamal and Ali. 'My dad has been hurt and they are not coming. Mum says we should go to Greece.'

'Oh,' says Kamal. He shakes his head. 'That won't be easy.'

'How do we get there?' asks Ali.

They both look at me.

I stare back and then I say, 'We got here, didn't we? So we'll get to Greece.'

We all bump fists and Ali shouts, 'Let the Force be with us!'

But my heart has sunk as low as the sun at bedtime. It must be 1,000 km across Turkey to the sea. We can't walk, can we?

# FIVE

## Escape!

**The Fun Girls**

- Where is Yasmin? She hasn't been to school
- Fatima B says they've run away
- Wish I could go
- My cousin's in England. He says it's so cool 😊

33

- Mmmm … you get free wifi
  and all the music you want 🤢

I AM SO HOMESICK!!!

I want my bed and my friends
and my school and Mum's cooking.

I have to find a way out of this
stinking camp to Greece.

We've been here six whole days
and I'm SICK of it.

Kamal wants to come with us.
That would be good. He's knows
how to find food and he keeps Ali
happy. I like talking to Kamal
about our lives back in Syria. He
misses his friends too.

What would Mum and Dad say about me, talking to him?

But hey! I know what *The Fun Girls* would say.

- He's fit!
- Go for it Yas.
- Has he got a brother? 😛

'Yas! Over here!' It's Ali.

I sent him to have a wash at the tap, but now he's talking to a man with a nasty face.

I go over and grab his hand.

'Wait!' says the man. He has a nasty voice too. 'You want to go to Greece? I can take you.'

'Be careful, Yasmin.'

It's Kamal, standing close to me and Ali.

He's right. There are a lot of bad men in the camp. But maybe it is time to take a chance.

'How much?' I say in a cold voice.

'Fifteen hundred dollars,' says the man.

Kamal laughs. 'You are mad!'

'Listen,' says the man. 'It is 960 km to the sea. I take you in a truck and then a boat to Greece. Good deal.'

Kamal looks away. He has no money. But I do.

'Thirteen hundred to take the three of us, or we talk to someone else,' I say.

The man grunts. I sniff and turn to walk off.

'OK, OK,' says the man.

I give him the money from the belt. There is still fifty dollars left. We will need that in Greece.

We meet the man by the gate at midnight. There are a lot of people.

The man takes us out of the camp and to a truck. Inside it is hot and we are all crushed together as the truck drives off.

'Do you think your mum and dad will get to Greece?' asks Kamal.

'They must,' I say, glad that Ali

is asleep now. 'What about your family?'

'Mum, Dad and my sister are dead,' says Kamal. 'I am alone.'

His big eyes are so sad.

I take his hand and say, 'We are here.'

His hand feels very soft. He does not let go.

I can hear *The Fun Girls* say,

He likes you Yas, do you like him?

*Yes*, I think.


It takes two days to get to the sea. When the truck stops we get down, tired and thirsty. The fresh air is so good.

'Walk that way,' says the man, calling from the truck. 'You will find the boat.'

'Hey!' a tall man calls. 'We cannot sail a boat!'

But the man drives off.

'What do we do now?' wails a woman holding a baby.

'We go on,' I say, and people nod and agree.

I take Ali's hand and Kamal takes my bag.

We have to climb over a rocky hill and then down a steep path to the beach. There is a rubber dinghy on the beach.

I hear the tall man say, 'It's too small for all of us.'

'Will ISIS come to get us, Daddy?' a little boy asks.

People mutter to each other. Everyone is scared, but we can't stay here.

'Come on,' I say. 'Let's get to Greece. It isn't far now.'

'Good for you,' says Kamal, and someone cheers.
We all walk across the sand and help each other into the boat.

The sea is choppy as we push off and sail away. The boat is very low in the water, but we sail on and on.

I begin to think, *This is OK, we can do it, we will get there.*

Then someone shouts, 'There's a hole!'

Suddenly water comes all over our feet.

Ali is screaming, 'Yasmin, save me, save me.' He clings to my neck.

Then the boat sinks and we are all in the water. My head goes under and I fight back up, gasping for breath. The water is so cold.

But where is Ali?!?

# SIX

## Now I Have Nothing

I swim and swim looking for Ali, but I don't find him.

I get to a beach. It is very dark, but I drag myself out of the water and fall down. My eyes close and I go to sleep.

I wake up with the sun on my face.
My feet are bare and so is my head.

No bag, no phone, no shoes, no
*hijab*, no money belt. Nothing!

I look around but I cannot see
Ali or Kamal. People are lying in
the sand. Are they dead? Is Ali
dead? What will I say to Mum and
Dad?

Tears fall down my face and
I shake all over.


An old woman calls to me. 'Walk
with us to the town. Come on, girl.
Get up!'

*OK,* I think. *Maybe Ali and*

*Kamal are in town looking for me.*

We go up the beach to a road.
My bare feet hurt as I walk.

Someone says, 'This is Kos, a
Greek island.'

Lots of people are sitting under
trees and I see some shops.

A man shouts from a car
window, 'Go home, migrants!'

The old woman says, 'They
don't want us here.' She shakes her
head.


I look for Ali and Kamal. There
are so many people; men in torn
shirts, a girl in a wheelchair,
children with dirty faces, teenagers

like me – and no one has any
shoes.

Where is Ali? I cannot lose him.
Not now.

Then I hear a loud scream and
a voice cries out, 'Yas! Yas!
Yasmin!!!!'

It's Ali!!!

Kamal is holding his hand.
They run up and Ali throws
himself on me. We are both crying.

'I lost my Jedi,' says Ali. 'But
Kamal saved me in the sea.'

'Thank you, oh thank you,'
I sob, as Kamal grins at us.

We are all together again, but now

what? We have lost everything.
I sit down under a tree, Ali on my
lap, and we fall asleep, worn out.

When we wake up Kamal hands us
a big plastic bag. Inside there is
water, sandwiches, fruit, flip-flops,
a white scarf for me and T-shirts.

'Where did you get this?' I say,
amazed.

Kamal grins. 'Women from
Greece and Germany are giving
them out. They are sorry for us.
Great, isn't it?'

We are so hungry we eat
everything. I cover my hair again
and feel so much better. A good

Muslim girl does not go out
without a *hijab*. Kamal nods, so
I know he is a good boy too.

Ali has a clean T-shirt on. Mum
would be happy.

Mum!

'How can I ring home?' I say in
a panic. 'I lost my phone.'

'Me too,' says Kamal, his eyes
sad again.

I think for a minute and then
I say, 'Come on, show me these
nice women.'

Kamal leads the way. There is a
small white tent by the shops.
Inside there are some women
handing out food. I go up to one
who is Mum's age. I think she is

German and she has a kind face.

'Please,' I say in English. I only know a few words. 'Phone? Mum? Home?'

The woman nods and hands me her phone. I thank her and tap in Mum's number.

A fresh tear falls down my face when she answers.

'Yasmin! How is Ali? Where are you?'

'We are on Kos, Greece. When are you coming? How is Dad?'

Silence. *Now what?*

I wait and wait, and then Mum says, 'Daddy died. I'm so sorry. Listen Yasmin … '

'NO!' I scream. 'NO, NO, NO!'

48

Kamal takes the phone from me. He listens and nods and writes something down.

He says, 'You must go to your Aunty Selma in Germany. Here is the mobile number.'

But I cannot do anything. I slump down on the floor and cover my face with my hands.

It is over.

This is the end of the road.

# SEVEN

## Good Wi-fi

We have been on Kos for more than a week. Every day Kamal gets us food and takes Ali to a tent for the children. I sit under a tree and stare at nothing.

We are alone.

Dad is dead. Mum is not coming to find us. I don't even

want to eat, but Ali and Kamal
make me.

The German woman comes to visit
me. Her name is Ingrid.

She speaks to me in a kind
voice and tells me not to give up
hope. Ali needs me, she says. We
are young. We can make a new life
and wait for Mum.

She doesn't understand. I don't
care about anything now.

Then one morning Ingrid gives me
her phone. 'Wi-fi good today,' she
says.

I stare at the phone and then I open *What's App*. There are pages and pages of messages from The Fun Girls.

**The Fun Girls**
- Yasmin babes, we miss you
- We love you. You are the BEST Fun Girl ever
- If you are reading this ... MESSAGE US !!!
- We will NEVER NEVER NEVER forget you
- Be happy Yas!
- Yeah and send us pics of everything
- Like boys!!!
- Whoo hoo!!

- MISS YOU  LOVE YOU  MISS YOU
  LOVE YOU

Wow!! They have put up messages
like this every day. How could
I forget them, my best friends back
home in my old life in Syria?

I feel something good inside me
for the first time since we fell in the
sea.

I message back.

- Ali and me OK but Dad died 😢
- I miss you too but we will
  ALWAYS be friends and we will
  ALWAYS be The Fun Girls. One
  day Syria will be free and we
  will be together again.

- The Fun Girls just want to have FUN!!! 😛 😛 😛

A message comes straight back with a selfie of all the Fun Girls. They are all wearing the same green and gold *hijab* and they are waving to me. A big surge of happiness goes through me like a wave from the sea.

I stand up and smile at Ingrid.

She says, 'Good girl. You must have hope.'

I nod. 'Mum says we have to get to Germany. I will find a way.'

My voice sounds strong. I feel strong. We will make it now. We have to.

Then I see Kamal and Ali running across the grass. Ali is shouting, 'Yas! I got a Jedi! I got a Jedi!'

He flings himself onto me and waves a plastic toy in my face.

'The lady gave it to me. She says I can keep it. Can I Yas? Can I?'

We are all laughing and I say, 'Yes, of course you can.'

'Let the Force be with us,' says Kamal with a grin, and we all bump fists.

Now I have to find the Force to get us to Germany and start our new lives properly.

# EIGHT

## Room for Two

I have been helping in the children's tent for a week. Ali has made a lot of friends, but we don't see Kamal all day.

Maybe he has new friends too. I am glad but also sad.

Ingrid lets me use her phone sometimes to read *The Fun Girls'* messages.

But this morning she is not there. Another woman tells me Ingrid is leaving. She is packing her car.

I feel tears in my eyes. I am going to lose another friend and I still don't know how to get to Germany.

I go outside and look for Ingrid. She is putting some bags into the boot of a red Golf.

'Hi,' I say and a tear falls down my cheek.

'Yasmin. Good, very good,' says Ingrid and she shuts the boot.

'Thank you for helping us and goodbye,' I say with a sob.

'No, not goodbye,' says Ingrid and she is smiling. 'You and Ali come with me. To Germany. Aunty Selma. Yes?'

I stare at her.

Did she really say that?

I can't believe it.

'But … well … oh thank you, thank you so much!' I say.

'Find Ali,' says Ingrid. 'Bring your bags. We leave in one hour.'

I turn to go and then I stop. What about Kamal?

If I ask about Kamal maybe Ingrid won't take any of us. But he has done so much for me and he saved Ali's life.

'Can Kamal come too?' I say.

Ingrid shakes her head. 'No room in car. Sorry Yasmin. He is big, strong boy. He can walk.'

I turn away and my legs are shaking. Mum says I have to look after Ali, but Kamal has been such a good friend. I feel so mean.

I look all over town and then I see Kamal outside a kebab shop. He is with some Syrian boys. I have to talk to him, but I feel shy.

'Kamal,' I say, in a soft voice.

He turns and looks at me.

Then he says something to the boys and comes over.

'OK?' he says.

I nod. 'Ingrid says she will drive me and Ali to Germany. We leave very soon and … '

' … there is no room for me,' he says, and stares at me with his sad eyes.

I stare back and then he grins.

'It's OK, Yas,' he says. 'Me and my mates are off too. We're walking to Germany. Might take a bit longer, but we don't care.'

I say. 'I'm so sorry. You saved Ali's life and got us food and … and … we … I will miss you.'

His eyes are very big as he stares at me and I tingle all over.

Then he says, 'I will find you,

Yas.' He puts a piece of paper in my hand.

Then he leans over and kisses me on the cheek.

The boys hoot and yell, 'Hey Kamal, man, time to go!'

He turns and walks away.

I stare after him in a daze and then I go to find Ali.

We rush around saying goodbye and packing.

Ingrid puts us in the car crammed with bags.

Then we are driving north.

I sit back and open Kamal's paper.

61

He has written his phone number and email address.

I will see him again, I think, and I laugh out loud.

Ingrid starts to laugh too and Ali shouts, 'My Jedi is laughing, Yasmin!'

How mad is that?

We are going to Germany – and a new life.

I can phone Mum when we get there and she will be so happy.

I know she will find a way to come to us.

And Hey!

I just had my first proper boyfriend kiss.

I can't wait to tell *The Fun Girls*!

Miriam Halahmy writes novels, short stories and poetry for children, teens and adults. She has a particular interest in refugees and asylum seekers, and has helped them to record their stories in writing workshops.

Her novel, HIDDEN, (Albury Books) tells the story of two teens who pull an asylum seeker out of the sea and hide him to save him from being deported. HIDDEN was nominated for the Carnegie medal and is currently being dramatised.

When not writing Miriam is very busy with her family, but she loves travelling and picking up different languages.

www.miriamhalahmy.com